HEART OF A COWGIRL

LACY WILLIAMS

"*I* see they let any old trash in here."

Weston Moore heard the words and knew they were directed at him. He worked at keeping an implacable expression on his face even as his temper simmered. His buddy Maddox's New Years' Eve party wasn't the place to air old business.

He turned to face the man who'd spoken. "Ezra." He stuck out his hand. "It's been a long time."

Not long enough, apparently. Weston's outstretched hand went ignored, and finally he dropped it.

Had Ezra approached just to insult Weston? He'd known the now-high school principal over a decade ago, but since Weston's return to Redbud Trails a few months earlier, they'd managed avoid each other.

Weston met Ezra's stare head on. He was four or five years older than Weston's thirty-three, and obviously, those old family grudges had never been resolved.

"Hey, man."

Maddox Michaels came from the crowded front hallway and clapped Weston's shoulder. He gave Ezra a nod. There was no way Maddox had missed the tension between the two. Maybe that's why he'd come over.

"I heard your season went well," Ezra said to Maddox, who was the junior high's football coach.

"We definitely missed having Jeremy on the roster," Maddox returned. "I bet Coach Franks loves having him on the team." Franks was the high school varsity coach. Ezra's son must have been a sophomore if he'd made varsity.

"You guys okay over here?" Maddox looked from one man to the other. "Need a drink or anything?"

Weston was reminded that Maddox was new on the school payroll. Junior high might be in a different building than the high school, but Weston wouldn't do anything to jeopardize his bud's career—if Ezra tried to start something.

"Everything's fine," Weston said.

Ezra drifted away to talk to someone else in the crowded living room. Maddox turned raised eyebrows on Weston, but he only shrugged his friend off with a smile.

You can't go home again.

Weston vaguely remembered some famous book with the title in a long-ago college literature class, and obviously it was true. He felt battered from the exchange with Ezra, but he wouldn't let it show.

He shouldn't have come.

The New Year's Eve party was in full swing, people

talking to each other, eating from the spread Maddox's wife Haley had laid out in the kitchen.

Weston didn't belong.

He'd left town a month after high school graduation, and he hadn't looked back.

Until he'd had no choice but to return three months ago, thanks to a frantic phone call from one of his twin sisters.

Maddox had pushed him to come to the party tonight. Knowing he was heading back to the city soon, Weston had done his best not to make new ties, but Maddox wouldn't be denied.

They'd always been seated next to each other back in high school, at least when the teachers had used alphabetical seating charts. But they'd been on opposite ends of the social spectrum—Maddox, the beloved football star, and Weston, barely eking out an education.

After Weston's return to town, Maddox had struck up a conversation with him in the church parking lot and then insisted Weston come to his early morning Bible study, which they had every week. Between Maddox and another new friend, Ben Taylor, Weston was surrounded by good men, good friends.

He'd hoped that things could change with folks in town. But if Ezra were any indication, the folks in Redbud Trails had long memories.

And Weston would be better off when he got home to Oklahoma City. It wouldn't be long now. Maybe another two months.

He'd miss his sisters. They were the only ones who

could've brought him back here to the town that despised him.

He shook himself out of his funk. So much for enjoying the party. He made a circuit of the room and couldn't help but notice a cute blonde shooting him covert glances from where she stood near the fireplace.

He'd seen her around town. Knew she must have some kind of retail business on Main Street, because she seemed to be there all the time. She'd had as many hairdos as the weeks he'd been here. Purple, red, pink.

Tonight's blond curlicues seemed kind of tame for her. But maybe the flirty red dress beneath a stylishly faded jean jacket was wild enough, because he couldn't keep his gaze from following her around the room.

She was pretty, no doubt. But he wouldn't do more than look. He didn't need a Redbud Trails complication. Especially in light of the way folks around here held grudges.

Besides, he was still licking his wounds after his last relationship detonated over the summer. He'd been looking for the one since...well, it seemed like forever.

The chances that he would meet her in Redbud Trails?

Zilch.

Still, something inside Weston chanted let's have some fun! He couldn't place this gal from his past. She must be a transplant. Which meant she might not know about the things that had chased him out of town.

He could have all the fun he wanted with her.

Yeah, right.

For some reason, the sensible part of him wasn't getting a word in edgewise as fun Weston tracked her progress across the room.

She started in a triangle with two other very attractive women in what seemed like an intense conversation. Didn't stop her from darting quick looks in his direction.

Ben Taylor and a man he didn't know came and claimed the other two, and the blonde bombshell slipped away, circling the room. She stopped to talk to an older couple, animated, showing off her dress. She was closer now.

And those looks were getting more frequent. And of longer duration.

He shouldn't encourage her. If she was grounded in her life here in Redbud Trails, there would be no future with her.

But the stupid part of him sent his feet wheeling into the empty farmhouse kitchen. With the overhead lights off and only a small light above the sink, the room was darker. Too intimate.

He heard the soft click of her boot against the wood grain floor. Closer.

Finally, he turned.

"Hi." She sounded shy for someone bold enough to chase him in here.

"Hey."

She was even more beautiful up close, with startling violet eyes. Could that even be her natural eye color? The end of her nose turned up the slightest bit. And she had a smattering of freckles.

His throat had gone dry. He cleared it. "Great party, huh?"

"Yeah." She looked back over her shoulder where the noise of the party still went on. No one seemed to have noticed them both slip in here.

She wore a blue-green scarf twined around her neck. It had dangly beads that clicked softly when she moved. She was over a foot shorter than his six-two, and slender.

Everything about her interested him, and that was dangerous indeed.

"I'm Weston." He stuck out his hand, and she gave hers. Thank God, not a repeat of earlier.

Her slim, cool hand disappeared entirely in his huge paw, and sparks skittered up his arm and down the back of his neck.

"I know." A mottled pink blush climbed her throat above that scarf and made its way into her cheeks.

His stomach hollowed out. What did that mean? I know.

"I'm Melody Carter."

Melody. It fit her. Her voice was a soft alto that he knew he'd be hearing in his dreams tonight.

"I wondered if you..." She faltered. Must've shored up her courage, because her shoulders straightened beneath that jean jacket. "Would you like to go out sometime? On a...date?"

The last word seemed almost to strangle her.

It was cute.

The women in Oklahoma City would eat her for lunch. She was entirely too sweet. He was used to the urban dating scene, women who weren't afraid to let a guy know what they wanted.

He really wanted to say yes. But she'd hit some kind of warning gong inside him a moment ago, and he hesitated.

Long enough for her to rush on. "I don't know if you're in town for very long, but that's okay, because I'm not looking for anything serious, and I know you must..."

Her words had tumbled over each other until they ground to an awkward halt. Her eyes had gone wide, and he didn't want to know what his expression looked like. Black. Ugly.

I'm not looking for anything serious. I know you aren't either.

Words that cut. Words that took him right back to his senior year in high school. When whispers had followed him around the hallways. When he'd skipped his commencement ceremony because it was too painful.

"I'm not interested." He probably should've attempted some semblance of politeness, but the words emerged harsh.

She took a step back, her eyes huge and locked on his face. She turned and fled.

You can never go home again.

He'd thought after fifteen years that people would be able to forget his reputation, but apparently he'd been wrong.

He couldn't wait to get back to the city where he belonged and forget about Redbud Trails. For the second time.

7

"STUPID, STUPID, STUPID."

Melody Carter took the stairs two at a time, desperate for a place to lick her wounds.

Don't cry, don't cry, don't cry.

The upstairs hallway was blessedly empty and mostly dark, the sounds from the party muted. Five doors led off from the hall. Which one was the bathroom?

A hiccuping sob stuck behind her breastbone, and she stopped with one hand on the wall. What if there were someone in the bathroom? She didn't want to be a crying mess if she ran into someone coming out.

She was already embarrassed enough.

So much for tackling number one on her bucket list. She blinked at the hot prickling burning her eyes, but it didn't erase the image of the sneer that had turned Weston Moore's handsome face into something altogether different.

She didn't have much experience with men—okay, any experience with men—but she hadn't thought asking one out was that big of a faux pas.

Maybe it was her.

There was movement behind her at the base of the stairs and, still not wanting anyone to witness her humiliation, she ducked into the first room.

But instead of finding a dark bedroom, the lights were on and a TV blared in one corner, showing the New York City countdown from the east coast. The room was full of kids. She must've been really upset not to notice the noise from the hall.

If it was only eleven o'clock, that meant she had to stay at the party at least another hour.

If she knew anything about being rejected, it was that you couldn't slink off in a corner or go home. She would have to act like the life of the party.

Even if she really wanted to go home and eat a tub of Cherry Garcia ice cream.

"Hiya, Melody!" Mikey, Anna's eight-year-old son, dropped the handheld video game he'd been engrossed in and bounced up off the bed, where he'd been sitting next to Livy Michaels.

"Melody!" Mikey's little sister Gina abandoned a pair of blonde dress-up dolls and threw herself at Melody, wrapping little arms around her knees until Melody wobbled.

Two teen girls—they must have been about fourteen —glanced her way from where they lounged on a pair of beanbags in the corner of the room.

On closer inspection, they had to be twins. One had her hair cropped short and wore baggie jeans and a T-shirt, while the other's hair was longer and had been curled around her shoulders. Still, their facial features were an exact match to each other's.

The girl with shorter hair wrinkled her nose and went back to the sports magazine she had spread across her knees, but her twin swiveled to face Melody, who felt caught between her own feelings and the exuberance of the children.

"You're her," she said excitedly.

"I'm...?"

Before the girl could answer, a childish shout echoed down the hallway, and something banged into the wall from outside the bedroom.

"What—?"

Both teen girls stood with identical long-suffering sighs. They brushed past Melody, who couldn't help watching.

In the doorway, they each caught a small boy in their arms.

"No wrestling," Pixie-cut said to the first.

"And no chasing," her twin said to the second.

"I can't believe you dragged me into this," Pixie-cut grumbled as they set the two small boys down. A third boy—triplets? Really?—darted between their legs, and the three boys ran circles around the room.

"Hey, you wanted the paycheck, too."

One of the boys picked up Gina's dolls and threw them at his brother.

"Those are mine!" Gina shouted.

The triplets scrabbled across the bed, knocking into Livy, who wobbled on the edge and then tumbled off.

She popped up almost immediately, her hair mussed. "I'm okay."

"We wanna play hide and seek!" one of the boys yelled.

Pixie-cut rolled her eyes but followed the boys out of the room.

"I'll play," Livy echoed, and Mikey rode her heels out

of the room too, leaving behind blessed quiet, Gina, and one twin.

"Sorry about that," the teen said. "We're sorta babysitting for the party."

Melody was surprised the younger children hadn't been put to bed, but then it would probably be impossible for them to sleep here with all the noise and distractions.

She hoped their mothers had a supply of patience—or another babysitter—for tomorrow morning.

"I'm Melody." She stuck out her hand, and the teen shook it rapidly, her eyes shining.

"You own the dress shop on Main Street. I love your clothes. I mean, the clothes in your store. But also what you're wearing is awesome. I mean..."

The girl shook her head, and a blush climbed in her cheeks, but Melody had a flash of pride—the same one she felt every time someone complimented her store.

"And you are...?" Melody knew all of her customers by name. It was one of the things she loved most about working and living in a small town. And she was sure she'd never seen this girl in her shop before.

"I'm Claire. And..." She waved her hand, indicating the hall or maybe the back of the house. "My sister is Chase. Actually, her real name is Charlotte, but she goes by Chase."

Chase. It seemed to somehow fit the other girl, with her short haircut and her tomboy outfit, but Melody couldn't help being curious as to why she'd chosen the moniker.

It didn't hurt that curiosity was a nice distraction from the disappointment and embarrassment still churning in her gut.

And she loved talking fashion.

"I have a brand new shipment of dresses coming in—a new designer I haven't carried before. Do you want to see some of them?" She plucked her smart phone out of her jacket pocket and pulled up her Photos app.

She'd fitted three mannequins with the new dresses, though she wouldn't change the display in the window until after her day off tomorrow. But she had taken pictures.

Claire's intake of breath told her all she needed to know as Melody swept her finger across the screen to reveal photos of the three dresses.

"I love that one," Claire said softly, her eyes locked on a knee-length navy dress in linen with a sweetheart neckline and a ruffled skirt. The lighter stitching made the dress.

"It would look great with your fair coloring. You should come in to the shop and try it on—"

A derisive snort from the doorway brought Melody's head up. Chase was there, standing half-hidden in the hallway but obviously eavesdropping. Claire stepped away from Melody, the interest disappearing from her face.

"I couldn't afford a dress like that," Claire said. But Melody heard the slight wistful undertone in her voice. Or maybe she'd imagined it. She'd been pretty sure there'd been at least some interest in

Weston's eyes tonight, and obviously, she'd imagined that.

"I run sales a lot," Melody offered. But not typically on her new inventory. She had to make a profit, or she couldn't afford to keep the store, even if she wanted to help a budding fashionista.

Claire's eyes tracked to Melody's phone, now casually at her side.

She hadn't mistaken the girl's interest. And if anyone knew about being denied what they wanted, it was Melody. Maybe it made her a softie.

But she was who she was.

"Actually..." she said slowly, an idea taking shape. She trusted her gut. This was the right thing to do. "I've been looking for a part-time employee and haven't found anyone. You could work for me a couple of days a week after school. Employees get a discount."

Claire's face lit, her expressive eyes dancing.

"We aren't sixteen," Chase said.

Claire didn't seem fazed. "Arianna Mills has a job, and she's the same age as us."

Melody nodded. "You have to get someone from the school to sign off on it."

"You know he'll never let you," Chase hissed from the hallway.

Some of Claire's excitement faded.

"Your dad?" Melody asked.

"Our brother," Claire said, her voice now subdued.

"Is he here? I could talk to him." Melody pressed. Something inside her knew that this was just right. She had been looking for help. A couple of hours away from running the register would allow her more time to work on the website and build her online presence—something that helped supplement her monthly income. If she relied solely on the customers in the tiny town of Redbud Trails, she's starve to death.

"What are you girls cooking up...?"

It couldn't be.

But of course, because that was the kind of night she was having, Weston Moore filled the doorway with his broad chambray-covered shoulders.

The smile on his face faded when he recognized her.

"This is our brother, Weston," Claire introduced brightly, somehow missing the tension that had Melody grinding her molars together.

The girl's glance ping-ponged between Weston and Melody, and her gaze turned almost pleading.

Maybe she hadn't missed the tension after all.

CHAPTER 2

*L*ive with abandon.

Puff, puff. January first wasn't cold enough for Melody's breath to make clouds in front of her, which was a good thing, or she might not be doing this.

First day of the rest of your life.

She kept her eyes focused on the lightening sky at the horizon, tried to concentrate on each breath of fresh air.

Her running shoes slapped against the gravel road heading out of town. The bungalows had given way to long stretches of winter grass with an occasional farmhouse. The words of her favorite Christian pop songs played through her mind, reminding her why she was doing this, working on another item on her bucket list.

Because this was so not fun.

Maybe she should have left off run a marathon.

But there was a part of her that reveled in the exertion, in the sweat rolling down her back.

Because she could do it. She was physically capable. And she hadn't always been.

A mile back, she'd unzipped the jacket she'd thrown on over her tank top and running pants—something she'd normally never do, but no one was out this early on New Year's. And who would've expected it to be almost fifty degrees in the dead of winter?

Her song—the one she'd chosen as her mantra— circled back through her head. Maybe tomorrow she'd remember her headphones, so she could loop the song over and over.

She wanted to live with abandon.

But she wasn't sure she knew how. Her first try at doing something bold had blown up in her face last night with Weston.

When he'd come upstairs to check on his younger sisters, he'd seemed almost angry to find her talking to them, though he hadn't actually accused her of anything.

She didn't understand why a man would be angry that she'd asked him out. She'd tried to make it low pressure. Say she wasn't interested in something long-term. Didn't men want flings?

Although her two best friends had recently gotten engaged—and Anna's wedding was coming up in six weeks—Melody couldn't imagine being with someone for the rest of her life.

Maybe because she was just now learning to live independently.

She knew her parents meant well, but their constant overprotectiveness had done plenty of damage. It had taken her going to an out-of-state college and months of therapy to understand the unhealthy relationship that had been cultivated. And the fear that still dogged her sometimes.

That fear was the reason she'd set up shop so far from home—a good three hours from her parents—and why she stayed, even when anxiety tried to get the best of her.

Her running shoes crunched on a different material, and she looked down. She hadn't been paying attention, wrapped up in her own thoughts. She didn't recognize this farm lane that had changed from gravel to dirt in the last several yards.

A farmhouse stood not far off the road. The barbed wire fencing was falling down, and long grasses had grown up, giving the place a slightly dilapidated look, though a new black truck was parked beside the house.

She slowed to a walk and glanced at the combo pedometer and GPS at her wrist. Six miles. And she wasn't doubled over in pain. She even thought she could get back to town at a decent pace.

Maybe a marathon was in her future.

And then the cramp hit.

FROM HIS VANTAGE point along the fence line, Weston saw the jogger approaching. Even from a distance, he knew it was a woman—couldn't help appreciating the slender shape, even if he couldn't make out her face.

Who was running out here?

Joggers, runners, dog walkers. He saw them all the

time near his downtown condo in the city, but in Redbud Trails? Not so much.

He paused to appreciate the graceful economy of her movement as she jogged by, then returned to his work.

He worked the posthole diggers into the hard winter soil again, keeping the runner in his peripheral vision.

The fence was falling down. It should've been replaced years ago. The whole property should've been replaced.

He wasn't used to this kind of work anymore. He kept himself fit by hitting the gym weekday mornings, but maybe he'd been sitting at a desk too much, because he was sweating through his long-sleeved T-shirt, and he'd barely begun.

He still had the entire fence line to go. He would've ignored it, but his buddy Ben Taylor had a barn full of rescued horses—animals that had been neglected or abused—and had asked Weston to board a couple of the animals. The question had been presented in front of his sisters, who'd immediately jumped on the idea and ran with it before Weston had agreed.

He hadn't been able to deny them, not when they'd turned those puppy dog eyes on him. He'd been manipulated by the girls, again. But how could he have turned them down?

They'd known their share of hardships. At fourteen, they were probably more grown up than they should have been, just like him. Growing up fast was required when one lived with Karly Moore.

He just wished he'd known how much work it would

be to get the property ready for animals again before he'd agreed.

The runner slowed to a walk near the rutted driveway that needed to be graded. Probably turning around.

And then she went down. Looked like she fainted.

Suddenly aware of how far out of town they were, his heart pounded. He left the posthole diggers behind and rushed toward her. When he got close, he jumped the ditch, his boots making little puffs of dust on the dirt road.

She wasn't out cold. She sat up, propping herself up with one hand while the other reached toward her leg.

Relief pounded through him as he crossed the last few feet to her. He was about to call out when he caught sight of her face.

Melody Carter again.

What the heck? Memories of last night and how much he'd wanted to say yes to her pressed in on him and made his voice a growl.

"What are you doing out here? You stalking me or something?"

Her head jerked up, her eyes widening almost comically. She must be in pain if she hadn't heard his approach.

A flush spread up her collarbone and into her neck, leaving a pale white line exposed. A perfectly straight line of scar tissue, just above the collar of her tank top.

"I'm on the road. It's a free country," she snapped. Her mouth was lined and pinched white. She was in pain.

And that made him feel like a heel. "What's wrong?" He squatted, coming down to her level.

"I didn't even know you lived out here," she muttered. Her head was down, and her fingers probed at her thigh.

"What's wrong?" he repeated. "Do I need to call for help?"

He prayed it wasn't anything vital, but he couldn't help but wonder about that scar across her collarbone. The volunteer fire department, with a paramedic on board, would take awhile to get this far out.

"It's just a cramp," she muttered again. He thought he heard *go away* emerge from between her clenched teeth, but he couldn't be sure.

"You sure? Are you even supposed to be running?"

She looked up at him, her brows drawn in confusion.

He pointed to the scar.

The pink blush that stained her face turned crimson, and she forgot about rubbing her leg as both hands reached for the zipper of her open sweatshirt.

"Hey," he said when her fingers fumbled.

She ignored him.

She must've been running awhile, because her sweat had combined with the dirt from the road, and she was getting grubby fingerprints all over her black sweatshirt in her hurry to zip it up.

When it was closed so tightly it might have choked her, she used both hands to push up off the ground.

He was too close and had to straighten and step back or get knocked onto his rump. He stepped back.

"I'm fine," she said through gritted teeth. She favored her right leg.

"I can see that."

She wobbled, and he shook his head at her stubborn independence. When she glared at him, he raised his eyebrows and his shoulders. What?

And then her face crumpled. She wobbled again, this time reaching out with both hands.

He caught her hands in his. The thought of her bursting into tears terrified him.

"What do you need?" he asked.

"Just hold me up for a minute." Her snappish tone and even her embarrassment had disappeared in the pain.

She released her grip on one of his hands, and he stepped closer in case he needed to grab her. She hissed as she reached down and grabbed the ankle of her injured leg, pulling her shoe nearly to her derrière in a stretch he recognized from his time at the gym.

"That helping?"

She shook her head, biting her lips.

From this close, he could see the tears standing in her eyes, though she was keeping them at bay for the moment. He could also see the rim of her contact lenses.

He'd thought her eyes had been unique. They'd certainly given him a punch in the gut. Was violet even her natural color?

She lowered her head, letting her forehead rest on his chest for the briefest moment. It was enough to knock off the headband that had kept her crazy curls out of her face. The headband slipped down around her neck and her curls burst free.

"Pink?" he asked.

There was a single hank of pink hair right in front. Her bangs maybe. It hadn't been there last night.

She glared at him, which probably didn't have the effect she was going for, since she still had tears standing in her eyes.

"I did it last night after I got home from the party." She said the words almost like a dare. Like she wanted him to comment about her hair or the party or something, but he'd spent enough time with his sisters the last few months to know when to keep his trap shut with an emotional woman.

"I like to change my hair to suit my mood."

"I've noticed." He'd seen her sporting a bright, unnatural shade of red once. Once she had a streak of green through her hair.

He found all of her looks cute. But couldn't help wondering...

"What's your natural color?" he asked, because it seemed weird not to make conversation considering they were standing so close, he could smell her toothpaste when she exhaled.

She shrugged. Not telling him.

She released her leg, and her foot dropped to the ground. She took his empty hand again and moved into a squat.

He pretended he felt nothing when they touched.

But Melody Carter was a whole lot of complicated.

And while normally he liked a challenge, a complicated woman in Redbud Trails—that was more challenge than he was willing to suffer.

He'd been there before. And he wasn't going back.

WESTON HAD BEEN silent long enough that Melody started to squirm.

She hadn't thought she could be more uncomfortable.

Was there such a thing as dying of humiliation?

He'd seen her scar.

She took such pains to keep it concealed, and of all the people in town, he had to see it. The person she'd humiliated herself in front of.

Okay, and the first guy that she'd been attracted to in years.

Talk about humiliating.

The cramp in her quad loosened, and she was able to take her first full breath in five minutes. She shook her leg out slightly and let go of Weston's hands.

Humiliation multiplier: she liked holding his hands. He had a strong, sure grip. Like he was a confident guy.

Too bad he wasn't interested in her and, now that he'd seen her scar, he never would be. Getting a glimpse of her scar had sent past dates scurrying for the safety of a healthy woman.

"What're you doing running all the way out here anyway? You need a ride back to your car?"

She shook her head. No way was she extending the humiliation.

"I'm training for a marathon," she said grudgingly. "And I'm fine."

"A marathon?" At the lilt in his voice, she couldn't help but look up.

Was that admiration in his gaze? "When?"

"When I'm ready."

Some of the admiration faded at her hedging.

"It's on the list," she said with a shrug. She didn't go around publicizing the list, but it wasn't a secret either. Anna and Lila would get a laugh out of the fact that she'd actually written down her list, since they often teased her about her OCD tendencies.

"Like your New Years' resolutions?" His lips twisted like he disdained that idea.

Not that she cared, but she corrected him anyway. "Like a bucket list. Things I want to do before I die."

His gaze slipped lower. Thank God she'd covered up with her jacket, even though she was sweating through it. "I thought you said—"

"There's nothing wrong with me. I just have a long list. It will probably take decades to get through it all."

There. That sounded brave. Bold.

Not like the scaredy cat she really was.

CHAPTER 3

$\mathcal{A}$fternoon sunlight slanted through the store's front windows. Three hours until closing. Main Street had been slow today.

Melody had kept her head down in the week since the disastrous New Year's Eve party and early morning non-injury. Too afraid to humiliate herself again.

She'd changed her running route, even though her normal, non-holiday schedule meant getting up to run at five a.m. before opening the store.

She hadn't had a chance to talk with Anna and Lila since the party, which was probably a blessing. Anna had been busy getting Mikey back into his school schedule and juggling wedding plans. Lila had been called on by the county to rescue a horse and had been scarce.

The bell over the front door jangled, and she looked up from the inventory report she'd been reconciling.

"Claire. Hi!"

"Hi." The teen came slowly over the threshold, looking around avidly, almost shyly.

Melody was proud of what she'd done with the store. It wasn't huge, but the wall racks and freestanding floor racks showed off the trendy clothes to their best advantage. The glass counter had a small selection of mid-range specialized jewelry locked inside, and a few smaller displays of costume jewelry took up space throughout the store.

Chase ducked through the door behind Claire with a second jangle of the bell.

"Hi, there!" Melody said in surprise.

Chase only grunted. Although she couldn't hide how her gaze tracked the room like her sister's had. Same as the last time she'd seen them, they were dressed completely differently. Claire wore a trendy sweater, a cute knee-length skirt, and tall boots. Chase had on a baggy T-shirt and baggy jeans.

"What's up, you two?"

"Just hanging out after school."

A glance at the clock. She hadn't realized it was late enough in the day for school to have let out, but it was almost four.

Don't ask, don't ask.

"How's your brother?" The words slipped out anyway, much to Melody's consternation.

Chase looked over her shoulder from where she played with a counter display of beaded bracelets. "Why do you want to know?"

Claire glared at her sister, pink rising in her cheeks.

She offered an apologetic smile to Melody. "He had a meeting in Oklahoma City today. He'll be back by dinnertime."

She didn't even know what he did. Or why he'd come to Redbud Trails.

She watched Claire pass Chase, whispering something that Melody couldn't hear. Chase shook her head tightly. Claire circled several clothing racks and then moved close to the navy dress in the window display—the same one that she'd gushed over the night of the party.

"So what brings you in today?" Melody asked. "Seems like I heard there was a school dance coming up...?"

She'd been thrilled when a couple of other teenage girls had come in during the week and bought dresses to wear to the Valentine's Day dance. The fact that they'd shopped local and not gone down to Oklahoma City made her proud of the work she was doing. And she needed a little confidence booster after a mid-week phone call with her mother that had left her feeling down.

"Are you two going to the dance?"

Chase snorted, but Claire shot her another glare, then turned back to the rack of belts she was examining.

"Maybe...I don't know," Claire said.

"She wants Eli to ask her." Chase offered. Melody might have thought the girl was finally warming up to her—she had no idea why Chase was so cool toward her—if not for the one-up look Chase sent her sister.

Color rose in Claire's cheeks, but she didn't deny it. "Well, you'd like it if Jeremy Warren asked you."

Chase glowered.

Melody moved away from the counter and approached Claire where she stood gazing at the dress. The price tag that had previously been artfully tucked in the armpit dangled free. Claire must've looked at it.

"I still have an opening for a part time cashier," she said softly.

"Weston said I could get a job."

"He didn't say you could get this job," Chase muttered.

Melody ignored her, unable to deny the joy shining on Claire's face. "Hang on."

She went behind the counter, pulled out a blank employment application, and pushed it across the glass-topped counter to the girl. "Fill this out. I looked online. This is the form the school will have to sign. If your brother agrees, you can start on Monday."

Claire leaned across and threw her arms around Melody.

The edge of the counter cut into Melody's ribs, but she patted the girl's back.

She well remembered those tumultuous times, as well as what her parents had done to her. She would give the girl a chance.

If Weston agreed.

THURSDAY EVENING, Melody counted the beaded

bracelets on the countertop display for the third time. Thirty-two.

But the printed thirty-four still glared up at her from the inventory list lying face up next to the display. She made a practice of taking inventory once per quarter. Not only did it help with the books at year end, but when she reviewed the sales reports, it helped her see trends in what her customers were buying.

She'd always found misplaced items before. Sometimes customers carried clothing into another part of the store. Sometimes things fell behind the counter.

But she'd already scoured the store and straightened up, thanks to a slow afternoon.

She'd never had anything walk out of the store before.

The bell over the door jangled, and she looked up at the clock over the back counter. Five minutes until closing. Just what she needed, a last minute browser when she was already frustrated by two missing bracelets.

But when she turned to face the customer, she found instead a broad-shouldered cowboy with his feet apparently glued to the welcome mat just inside the doors.

Weston.

His eyes flicked around, taking in the displays.

"Hey," she greeted.

His eyes came to rest on her, and one corner of his mouth kicked up in a smile. "Blue?"

One hand came to her hair, a flare of self-consciousness taking her by surprise. She forced her hand back down to rest on the counter.

She wasn't ashamed. She liked being able to do her hair how she wanted.

"The pink was starting to wash out," she said. Which was partially true. Her plain-Jane brown roots had started showing, and she'd had to re-dye the blonde. She liked being a blonde. They had more fun, right? Weston had been on her mind when she'd added the blue streak to her bangs.

"What can I do for you?"

He held up a piece of white paper, folded lengthwise.

She raised her eyebrows.

Finally, he started toward the register, skirting a rack of gauzy skirts like it was going to burn him.

"They're just clothes. They don't bite."

He leveled a look on her as he neared. "I spent the afternoon working in the barn. Don't want to get dust and who-knows-what all over your pretty things."

She appreciated that, though his T-shirt and faded jeans didn't appear dirty. The look on his face told her it was more than that. The frilly girl things made him uncomfortable. Out of his element.

At least he thought they were pretty. Not that that translated to him thinking she was pretty.

"Claire seemed to think I had to be the one to drop this off to you." He laid the paper on the counter in front of her.

Their hands brushed as she reached for it, and he jumped. Actually jumped. As if he couldn't stand the feel of her.

Piqued, she forced her gaze to stick to the paper and

stay away from the man. It was the application, of course. Why else would he be in her store?

"Great," she said past the knot in her throat. "I told her she could start Monday. Is two hours on Mondays, Wednesdays, and Fridays too much?"

"It sounds all right, as long as her schoolwork doesn't suffer."

She nodded, her eyes still on the counter. Expecting him to leave.

He didn't. She could feel the weight of his gaze on the top of her head. It prickled.

Finally he stepped back from the counter and she lifted her gaze. She couldn't read the look on his face.

"You sure you want Claire to work here?"

"Any reason I shouldn't?" Unwittingly, her mind went to those two missing bracelets. Claire and Chase had stood shoulder-to-shoulder next to the display before.

He shrugged. "She has no experience."

She remembered the girl's anticipation and the joy that had lit her face. "Everyone has to start somewhere, right?"

He took another long look around the store, his expression perplexed.

"Do you have a problem with my store?"

His eyes cut back to her. "Why would I?"

She kept her chin high. "I don't know." Maybe because he seemed to have a problem with her since the night they'd met. "You keep looking around like some of the clothes are going to jump off the rack and attack you or something."

That corner of his mouth lifted again—what would it take to earn a full-blown smile from the man?—and he stuck his hands in his front pockets.

"I guess I just don't get it."

"Don't get what?"

"Fashion. I mean...you look fine."

Fine. She looked down at her slim pencil skirt and sweater, which was brand new in her stock this year. Even her chunky heels and the clunky necklace had been chosen with care. Fine.

"I sell all of these pieces," she said, because she didn't know what to say. Why was he still here? Just to torture her? Embarrass her more?

His lips flatlined. He pushed a hand back through his hair. "Maybe I don't understand them."

Her brows raised this time.

He flapped one hand awkwardly in front of himself. "You. Women. The twins."

His consternation was so adorable that she could almost forgive him for declaring her simply fine.

"They're teenage girls." She stated the obvious. "They aren't meant to be understood. You just have to survive it."

Her words didn't seem to help. And then her curiosity got the better of her. "How did you come to be their guardian anyway?"

"Our mom had to go to rehab. I didn't know she'd been overdoing it on pain meds again until Chase called me, freaking out. She didn't want to go into the foster system."

Oh. She'd had no idea. "I don't blame her." Maybe that explained some of the girl's standoffishness. "So you came back to town. How long had you been gone?"

A muscle in his jaw ticked. "You mean you don't know the whole sordid story?"

WESTON STUFFED his hands back in his front pockets. He'd been shopping with girlfriends plenty of times, but he'd never felt as uncomfortable as he did right now, surrounded by Melody's stock.

Or maybe it was the look in her eyes.

She didn't know about his past.

So what had prompted her invitation at the New Years' party? Just looking for a fun time. He'd thought...

He shook those memories away. "I left town right out of high school."

"And haven't been back since?"

He nodded.

He didn't know why she'd taken an interest in Claire, but since she'd met Melody, his sister had gone from moody and quiet to bubbly and more like the little sister he remembered.

He should've spent more time with the girls. Had them down to the city more. He'd had good reason to stay away from Redbud Trails, but that shouldn't have meant he stayed away from his sisters.

He was still raw from the meeting with Ezra Warren earlier in the afternoon. Claire had needed a representative of the school to grant permission for her to work at the dress shop. It shouldn't have been a big deal, but Eve's brother had treated Weston with such contempt that he'd nearly lost his temper and slugged the guy.

After that, he'd sat in his truck in the parking lot for twenty minutes, trying to shake off the old despair. And the knowledge that Eve had never come clean with her family. Her brother—and probably her parents—still thought he was the loser who'd knocked her up.

He was tired of it all.

He realized he'd zoned out from Melody's last question. "Sorry." He rubbed the back of his neck. "It's been a long day."

She nodded, the smile she'd greeted him with now dimmed. "For me too. I was just wrapping up."

She moved toward the door, and he followed, aware of the brush of her shoulder against his bicep. He looked down on that piece of blue hair.

And had to remind himself that she was off-limits. She was Redbud Trails.

He wasn't.

As they approached the windows, he motioned to his motorcycle, parked at the curb. "You need a ride home?"

Her eyes flicked to it, and her brows lifted slightly. She shook her head.

"Riding a motorcycle isn't on your list?"

Now her eyes cut to his face. She shrugged. Shy, or had something he'd said earlier upset her?

"You scheduled that marathon yet?" he asked.

She bit her lip. "Not yet."

He gave another nod to the motorcycle. "So do you want to check something off your list today or what?"

She clicked the lock with a decisive thump. With him still on the inside. "I'll get my coat. Be right back."

She disappeared into what must be a storeroom in the back.

Leaving him with his heart thundering like he was back in high school again. He could only hope this wasn't a mistake.

CHAPTER 4

"I don't think this is the right one," Melody said as she emerged from the dressing room.

Four days had passed since Weston's appearance in her store. Today had been Claire's first day, and the girl had done well training on the register.

Now it was after hours, and the store was closed, so there was no one other than Anna and Lila to see, but she was still self-conscious of the scar that felt as if it glowed like a beacon above the sweetheart neckline of the pale pink bridesmaid's dress.

The front lights in the store had been turned off, leaving it dark, but the interior lights closest to the dressing room were on. She supposed someone could see inside if they were so inclined, but surely no one peering in from the street could see the scar.

She couldn't help laying her palm over it when Lila emerged from the second curtained dressing room and

Anna finally looked up from her cell phone. Apparently, there had been some minor emergency at home.

"I think it's okay," Lila said, attention on the triple mirror. She turned a slow circle. "If you like dresses."

But Anna's eyes zeroed in on Melody. "It's too low-cut?"

And then Lila turned, so they were both staring at her.

"Aw, it's not that bad," Lila said. Both women had seen the scar after the first dress—a horrid fuchsia affair.

"What about makeup?" Anna asked gently.

Melody's face burned. "It doesn't really...cover." The skin was translucent and made too much of a ridge for makeup to hide it.

She never showed her scar. Showing it now made her feel naked.

She didn't do naked.

"I think you're right about the pink. A Valentine's wedding should have red bridesmaid dresses, shouldn't it?" Anna stood.

"Anna, if you love the dress then I don't..." Melody inhaled deeply, the breath sawing through her chest. "I don't have to be a bridesmaid."

Anna shot her an incredulous look. She spun and headed toward a rack of knee-length dresses on a nearby display.

"Uhh—you aren't getting out of this," Lila said. "If I have to be a bridesmaid, you do too."

"Hey!" Anna protested, still hunting through the dresses on the rack.

"I want to do it." Melody rushed to reassure her friend. She'd never been a bridesmaid before. There were experiences here waiting for her, even if this wasn't officially on her list, it was something she desperately wanted. "It's just..."

Lila came close, tugging Melody's hand away from her breastbone. Heat prickled across Melody's skin at Lila's stare, and she knew her mottled color was showing off the scar even more.

"You can barely see it," Lila said. She tilted her head to one side. "Except when you blush like that."

Lila didn't ask where she'd gotten it. Small blessings.

"If my scar is visible, I'll be blushing like this the whole time. You guys are the only ones who have seen it. You and—"

She cut herself off. In her nervous chatter, she'd almost spilled the beans about seeing Weston that morning.

And of course, they noticed. Anna, with her arms full of crimson fabric, paused several feet away. Her entire being radiated curiosity.

"Us and who?" Lila pressed.

There would be no getting out of it now. After the way she'd nosed into their business when they were falling for their men, they'd already started ganging up on her about finding someone to love.

"Weston," Melody muttered, tugging her dress from Anna's arms. She retreated to her dressing room, but it was too much to hope that her friends wouldn't take the admission and turn it into some kind of drama.

"Weston Moore?" Lila asked, her voice floating over the partition between the two dressing rooms.

"That's the only Weston I know," Anna said. Her voice sounded more tight than curious. "What happened?"

Melody growled to herself as she pulled the pale pink confection off. "I was out running one morning—early— and I had a cramp and sat down to rest in his front yard."

If you could call the ditch in front of someone's property a yard.

"And I'd unzipped my jacket because I was hot and he saw." The last words tumbled from her lips in a rush.

"How did we not know this?" Anna's voice sounded muffled as Melody shimmied the red dress over her head.

"The only thing I heard was that he took her for a ride on his motorcycle," Lila said.

She didn't have to guess how they'd found out about that. Small-town grapevine.

"He gave me a ride home, that's all. His sister works for me. One of them. Claire."

"Is she babbling?" Lila asked.

Anna was noticeably silent.

Melody tuned Lila's voice out as she scrutinized the bodice of the dress. It had a square neckline at least two inches higher than the previous dress. And her scar was mercifully out of sight. But the knee-length flared just right on her. How would it fit Lila, who was several inches taller?

"Is it too short for you, Lila?" she asked as she pushed through the curtain.

Lila stood with one hand propped on her hip, wearing an expectant look. The dress looked great on her.

Anna's expression was more concerned than anything else.

"What?" Melody asked. She half-turned and glanced down the back of her dress in the mirrors.

"We want to know what's up with you and Weston," Lila said eagerly.

"Nothing." Melody spun in front of the triple mirror. She liked this one.

"That's probably a good thing," Anna said.

And Melody stopped spinning. Her chest caught at Anna's unexpected words. Anna, who'd been gung-ho for Lila to connect with Ben.

"What do you mean?" Lila asked.

Anna's eyes slid away in the mirror. She fiddled with a fold of her sleeve. "Just that Melody should be careful around him. His reputation back in high school was...well, it wasn't good."

Melody remembered the shadows in his eyes from the other night. How he hadn't been home since his high school graduation.

But something inside gravitated toward him, regardless of Anna's warning. "There's nothing going on. Like I said, he saw my scar."

"So?" Lila's tone indicated she didn't get it.

"So anytime a guy I like sees my scar, one of two things happens. They pity me. Or they get freaked out.

And Weston and I are barely acquaintances, which means nothing is going to happen."

Lila joined Melody in the mirror. "I think you should still go for it. So what if he saw your scar?"

Anna came up behind them both, giving Lila a pointed look before leaning down to straighten the back of Melody's skirt. "I still think you should be careful."

Melody tried to smile at the both of them in the mirror, but it didn't quite make it. She hadn't told them about Weston shutting her down at the party, and she wouldn't.

"I don't think so," she said, ending the conversation. For now, at least.

After Anna had declared the red dress the one and Melody had promised a shoe-shopping trip in the city next weekend, Melody considered their words as she locked up the shop.

She was attracted to Weston. And he'd seen her scar.

Lila was kind to say that it didn't matter. But the truth was, it did. Her scar—her surgery and her parents' lingering fear—had dictated her life up until her college days.

She didn't want it to dictate her life now. Couldn't go back to that.

So what if she'd felt something when Weston had let her off his bike the other night?

It didn't mean he didn't pity her.

CHAPTER 5

a week had passed since the bridesmaid's dress selection, and Melody was ringing up a late afternoon customer after an exhausting hour-long sales session with a persnickety woman when her cell buzzed in her pocket.

She didn't make a habit of answering her personal phone during business hours, but when it rang a second time only minutes later, she dug it out of the pocket of her skinny jeans.

The number wasn't programmed into her phone, but it was a local area code. She answered it.

"It's Weston. Are you busy?"

"Kind of. What's up?" And how did you get my number?

She glanced at the cart bearing a load of skirts and blouses from the new stock that had arrived yesterday. Then to the pile of inventory reports—showing four discrepancies now—and the accounts payable that she also needed to reconcile tonight.

She'd planned to play back video from the surveillance cameras after she closed the store for the day. Maybe she could see who was walking off with her merchandise.

"Something's going on with the girls. Claire—I think it was Claire—called me, and she was sobbing into the phone. Have you heard from her?"

"I haven't." Today was one of Claire's days off. Melody hadn't seen either of the girls, but neither had she expected to. Things had gone relatively smoothly so far with Claire working part time.

Weston sighed. "I'm in the city, about to walk into a meeting that I can't miss. Could you go check on them?"

She hesitated.

"I wouldn't ask, but..."

But maybe he had no one else. She couldn't help remembering Anna's warning. "They're at home?"

"Yeah, I got that much out of her."

"Nothing else?"

"It was something about a boy. I didn't understand it all—look, I've gotta go. Thanks, Mel."

She stared at her phone after he'd ended the call. Obviously, he trusted her enough to ask her to check on the girls. But why?

Or was she really the only person in town that would help? No, that didn't make sense. At the party, he'd been friendly with several of the guys.

Maybe it was because she understood Claire more than he did.

She glanced at the clock again. She had an hour to go until closing time, but if there was drama involving a boy, she'd better get to the bottom of it.

She texted Claire that Weston had called and that she was picking up Chinese food and would be there soon.

Boy trouble called for nothing less.

An hour and a half later, after making the drive to Weatherford and back, she knocked on the door of their farmhouse.

When Claire opened the door, she was dry-eyed.

It was Chase, sitting on the sofa with an empty box and numerous crumpled tissues around her.

"I brought comfort food," Melody offered, holding up the plastic bag.

Chase took one look at her and burst into tears all over again.

WESTON WALKED into the house just after eight to find three hysterical females sitting around the small nook table in the kitchen.

They had a spread of cardboard Chinese cartons open on the table—no plates—and Claire waved a pair of chopsticks wildly while Chase and Melody cackled with laughter.

Claire seemed fine.

And then he noticed Chase's red-rimmed eyes. What was going on? Between the two girls, Chase was normally more private with her emotions. What had upset her?

But he knew better than to rush in and demand answers.

"Y'all look like you're having fun," he said.

He received an assortment of greetings, from Melody's soft "hello," to Claire's chopstick wave and Chase's nod.

He plucked a half-full container of lo mein from the center of the table before he could get his hand swatted and retreated to lean against the counter near the kitchen sink. He pulled a fork from the drawer and dug in.

Where had the food come from? There wasn't a Chinese restaurant in tiny Redbud Trails. His gaze snagged on Melody, and when she caught him looking, he raised his eyebrows at her.

She wrinkled her nose and tuned back in to the girls' conversation, but pink crept into her cheeks.

It made him want to steal her away, just for himself.

"Then she dumps her entire tray of meatloaf and mashed potatoes on his lap."

"You could try that, but I bet you'd get detention." Melody pushed a carton away, as if she'd overdone it.

He felt a moment of relief. At least it wasn't one of his sister's who'd dumped food on some poor unsuspecting guy.

"What's going on?" he asked, deciding it was better to brave an emotional storm than stay in the dark.

Chase's lips trembled, and she clamped them together.

Claire put a hand on her shoulder. "Principal Warren changed the policy for the school dance. No freshmen are allowed to attend, even if an upperclassmen invites you."

That was the tragedy that had his normally-stoic sister in tears?

His cluelessness must've shown in his expression, because Chase burst out, "Everyone was talking about us at lunch. Saying that the rule got changed because of us."

He still wasn't tracking. "Because of you two, specifically?"

Just because rumors were flying didn't make them true. And he well knew how high school drama could unfold at the speed of light.

And then Claire's mention of Principal Warren broke through the jumble of his thoughts. Ezra Warren.

The policy hadn't been changed because of the twins. It was because of him. Because Ezra Warren still held a grudge.

It was just crazy enough to be true.

Chase sniffed, and Melody shook her head when he opened his mouth. He wasn't even sure what he would've said.

"I think the best way to get over it is a makeover," Melody said. "You might feel more confident—"

"Yeah, right." Chase glowered at her.

Melody fished in what must be her purse, which had been hanging off the chair behind her. She came up with a small pad of paper and a pencil and started sketching so fast, his eyes couldn't follow the lines on the page.

"How was your meeting?" Claire asked him.

"Fine." He didn't let his attention waver from Melody, but he saw Claire make a face at him in his peripheral vision.

Expectation—or maybe it was anticipation—hung in the room, everyone waiting to see how Chase would react to whatever Melody was sketching.

"I'm not into all the girly-girl frills like you and Claire," Chase said, but her eyes were glued to Melody's paper.

"You don't have to be." Melody swept her pencil across the paper and then flipped the pad around for the twins' perusal. He found himself stepping closer to see.

Chase gasped softly. Melody had drawn a girl with more than a passing resemblance to Chase in a pair of jeans that even he would recognize as trendy and a T-shirt that hugged the slender curves he tried really hard not to think about teenage boys thinking about. Some kind of chunky bracelet made the outfit more feminine than it should've been, especially with the ballet flats Melody had sketched.

"That's perfect for you," Claire said even as Chase shoved the notebook back toward Melody.

But not before he'd seen the flare of interest in her eyes.

"I can't afford anything like that, and even if I could, it doesn't matter." Chase shoved back from the table, her chair legs scraping against the floor.

Something else was going on. He could read his sisters pretty well by now, and the look they shared said it all.

"C'mon, Chase, you're being silly," Claire murmured.

"Don't say it," Chase said, pointing a shaking finger at her sister. "Look at Weston."

What? How was he involved? He'd just walked in.

Claire shot an apologetic glance at him and kept talking. "Just because Weston is unlucky in love—"

Chase started to say something, but Claire cut her off. "And mom. Just because the two of them have been unlucky in love doesn't mean our family is cursed."

"I'm not..." He shut up when Chase gave him a scathing glance.

"Eve. Do I need to say more than that?" The name hit him squarely in the gut, but not with the power it had once had over him. And Chase wasn't done. "Or what about the dozens of girlfriends since?"

Okay, now his face was getting hot. "There haven't been that many."

Movement from the corner of the room showed Melody reaching for her purse. Smart woman. The twins could go on for hours, and this wasn't her problem.

"Melody, wait!" Claire turned.

"Oh, just let her go home," Chase fumed. "It's not like she would help me if she knew what I'd done."

And suddenly, what he'd thought was a normal teenage drama-slash-spat was something more serious.

"What do you mean?" Melody put her purse on the chair she'd just vacated.

He set the now-empty carton on the counter, heart pounding. "I think you'd better explain, young lady."

But Melody's small hand on his forearm stalled him from stepping into Chase's personal space, his first instinct.

"It was you? Stealing from the store?" Melody asked.

What?

Claire gasped. "Why would you do that?"

Chase's face turned bright red. "Because."

"Because you wanted to get me fired?" Now Claire advanced on her sister, a dangerous look in her eyes. "What if Melody had thought it was me?"

A glance at Melody revealed a slightly guilt-ridden look, which she quickly blanked.

"I wanted to be pretty too!" Chase's outburst made all three of them freeze in place.

And then her face crumpled, and she bolted from the room.

What had just happened here?

He stood rooted in place, feeling helpless and frustrated and a whole mix of things.

Claire started to chase after her sister, but Melody reached out for her. "Let me go."

He put both hands on top of his head, his elbows stretching toward the ceiling. "I don't understand what just happened here."

"She likes Jeremy," Claire answered, as if that explained the whole thing.

It didn't.

MELODY KNOCKED at the threshold of what must be the twins' bedroom.

She was aware of Claire hovering behind her in the hallway, and she'd heard Weston bang out of the back door.

Inside the bedroom, twin beds were covered in colorful bedspreads. A small table was wedged between them. One half of the table had a single orderly stack of books, while the other had a messy jumble of magazines, nail polish, and papers.

Chase sat on the bed farther from the door, her arms wrapped around her knees. Behind her, a window was cracked, letting a slight amount of cold air into the stuffy room.

"You might not want to talk to me," Melody said. "But I won't press charges if you listen."

The teen hiked her chin, staring out the open window. Tears sparkled in her eyes.

"You might be barred from the school dance. But so what? You've got your friends. You've got Weston. Your brother loves you. He put his life in Oklahoma City on hold to come here and be with you and your sister."

"For how long?" Chase muttered. "He can't wait to get back to his real life."

The words muttered into her knees made a pang in Melody's gut.

"Whether you choose to be trendy or grunge or goth, your brother will still love you."

"And so will I." Claire bounced into the room and folded herself into a pretzel next to Chase on the bed.

Melody's heart warmed, seeing the two together. She'd wanted a sister so bad... "You don't have to be anything you don't want to be. But you do have to be yourself. Stop hiding."

Color rose high in Chase's cheeks. "You'd still help me, after I took stuff from your store? I still have it—in my backpack."

"I'll still help you." She showed the pad of paper that she'd held like a shield against her stomach. "I've got some jeans just like this at the store, but we'll have to search online if we want to find a jersey this cute."

Chase reached for the notepad, and Melody stepped closer, daring to perch on the corner of the bed. "Now, what's this about a curse...?"

Both girls looked slightly sheepish. It was Chase who spoke first. "Our mom was whining about one of her ex-boyfriends and said something about our family being cursed in love. Especially after Weston and Eve..."

Claire elbowed her sister. Chase looked up and must've caught sight of Melody's interest in her expression.

"He didn't do whatever everyone thinks he did," Claire said softly. "Mom spilled the beans once when she was...out of it."

High. Melody read between the lines.

Whatever had chased him out of town, he'd been innocent. She'd guessed as much. Hoped as much.

She still wanted to know what it was. Anna hadn't been specific when she'd warned Melody off.

And prying it out of the twins wouldn't be cool. Especially if he ever found out.

She could ask him straight out, but tonight, it felt as if they'd forged a tentative friendship. She couldn't risk ruining that, not when things had begun to get interesting.

CHAPTER 6

eston had just stepped off the porch and was making his way toward the barn when he heard giggles emerge from the cracked window.

The boulder in his gut dissipated slightly. Thank God Melody had been understanding about the theft. If she'd wanted, she could've pressed charges, and then where would the family be?

Melody constantly surprised him. She'd taken the girls' drama in stride and barely reacted to Chase's revelation.

Meanwhile, he felt like he was treading water in the middle of the ocean with no lifeboat in sight. In a hurricane.

He'd allowed the distance to grow between himself and the twins. After everything that had happened with Eve, it was easier to cut ties to Redbud Trails.

And now they were growing up, abandoned by their

mother and facing peer pressure and boy trouble, and he was woefully ill-equipped to deal with all of it.

He blew off some of his frustration mucking stalls for Ben's two mares. The gentle ladies had been severely neglected, but now they were putting on pounds they'd lost, building back muscle. In a few months, they'd be ready to go to new families, ones who would treat them right.

Or he and the girls could keep them.

The thought brought him up short as he bucked the wheelbarrow of manure into the compost pile out back.

He wasn't planning to stay in Redbud Trails long term.

He had a life back in Oklahoma City. A good life. A sweet condo, season tickets to the Thunder, plenty of friends to hang out with.

But the twins were here. Even after Mom got out of rehab, could he trust that she'd stay clean? The fact that he hadn't known in the first place that she was hooked on pain meds still upset him. He needed to make sure the twins were safe, and he couldn't do that adequately from the city.

And then there was Melody.

He didn't know her all that well, and he wanted to know more.

Footsteps crunching in the dry grass outside drew his attention toward the open barn door.

She was walking across the grass toward the barn as if his thoughts had conjured her. He shucked his gloves, ran one hand through his hair, and headed toward her.

WESTON MET Melody just outside the barn, beneath the flickering light from the nearby post. His jean jacket was open over his T-shirt, which clung to the flat planes of his stomach.

He ran one hand through his hair, muscles in his arm pressing against the material of his jacket.

Lines creased around his mouth. "I owe you for not pressing charges."

A gust of wind fluffed her scarf, and she quickly pressed it against her sternum.

"She returned the things she'd taken."

"Still. Let me take you out this weekend."

Tempting. Especially in the face of what she now knew. But she couldn't forget his expression when his eyes had locked on her scar that bright morning. "I don't date out of obligation."

Something sparked deep in his eyes.

"You didn't get Eve Warren pregnant."

Surprise flashed across his face, and then a frown flattened his lips. "I don't make a habit of talking about past mistakes."

Not exactly an answer. And apparently, he considered Eve a mistake. "Did you love her?"

He stepped closer to her, and the spark in his eyes changed to something more dangerous. Dangerous but not menacing.

She stood tall. Well, as tall as someone her height could stand.

"You want to get personal, let's talk about this." He flipped the ends of her scarf over her shoulder, revealing the scar.

He touched the very tip of his finger to her collarbone, just next to the ugly reminder.

She moved to tuck her scarf back down, knocking his hand aside.

"I don't make a habit of talking about it." Her words came out in a whisper.

"It's a shame." His voice had lowered too, maybe because he was so close. Either he'd edged closer, or she had. Only inches separated them. "Looks like a badge of courage to me."

And then he closed the distance between them, his hand moving up to cup her cheek, his fingers tunneling into the hair behind her ear.

She hadn't been expecting it, and it took a moment to register the shock of his lips, cool from being outdoors, as they met hers.

She pressed one hand against his chest and moved back slightly, surprised to find herself breathing nearly as hard as she did when she ran.

"I don't want you to kiss me because you feel sorry for me."

She hadn't pushed back far enough, because his breath was warm on her lips when he answered. "I don't."

He tugged her close again, his hand warm at her waist.

She met his kiss this time, tilting her head to change the angle and—oh! His lips slanted across hers, and heat flowed up from her toes and flushed all through her body.

She pulled back a second time.

Wobbled a little, so it was a good thing his arm had come fully around her waist now.

She had an up close and personal view when his lips stretched in a smile.

"I don't want you to kiss me because of obligation," she said.

"All right."

She saw the words form on his lips almost even before he spoke them.

She might be fixated. "Okay."

And this time, she rose on her tiptoes and instigated the kiss.

CHAPTER 7

The next morning, Melody stood in the kitchen of her little bungalow after her run. Sweat soaked the sweatshirt she wore over her tank top and running pants—she definitely wasn't going to show anyone else her scar—and she carefully stretched out her legs, holding on to the counter for balance. Her half-drunk green smoothie rested on the counter next to her open laptop.

She couldn't stop thinking about Weston and the kisses they'd shared.

Her first kiss, and it had been amazing. She wasn't sure anyone else's could compare.

And Weston was going to leave. The girls were sure of it.

It wasn't that far of a commute to the city, but with her long hours minding the store and his career, what kind of a long-distance relationship could they have?

When she wasn't focused on the best part of the

evening—he'd kissed her!—the mystery about Eve dogged her. She knew she shouldn't, but she grabbed her laptop, set it on the kitchen counter, and fired it up while she waited for her coffee to brew.

She clicked off the marathon registration site that came up first on her Internet browser. She'd almost clicked Register last night in a fit of madness before her courage had failed. Now she navigated to Google and typed Weston Moore and Oklahoma City into the browser.

He had a lot of hits.

Investment broker hits it big with local restaurant.

Oklahoma City's one hundred most eligible bachelors.

Weston Moore signs top-dollar deal.

The headlines went on and on.

He wasn't the failure a few spiteful folks in town had made him out to be. He might've left town under a cloud of suspicion—though she now believed those accusations had been fabricated—but he'd made something of himself.

He was the kind of man who returned to a place who'd scorned him to protect and take care of his sisters.

She saw so much more in him than what the folks in town believed him to be.

And she might be falling for him.

But what kind of future could they have?

She could understand why he didn't want to be in Redbud Trails. She didn't make a practice of listening to the gossip in town—with the notable exceptions of when Anna and Lila had been dating their respective beaus—but she could see how the lies told about him could follow him around. In her mind, it made perfect sense that Weston didn't want to live in the shadows of the past.

She just hoped her heart could learn to understand that, too.

EVENING WAS FALLING as Weston rubbed at the ache between his eyes, pushing back from the kitchen table where he'd been reviewing a contract for one of his clients. His brain was wiped and the legalese started to read like a foreign language.

He felt a little like a teenager, stuck inside too long doing homework.

Not that he'd spent all that much time on his homework when he'd actually been a teenager. He'd been busy with an after-school job that helped keep food on the table—and the mortgage paid. His little spare time had been spent with Eve.

But thinking about Eve didn't do him any good. He'd heard that she'd moved to Texas and married some guy. Probably had a passel of kids by now.

Some folks in town—like Ezra—seemed to want to remember the mistakes Weston had made in the past, but there were plenty of people—like Maddox Michaels and Melody—who judged him for the man he was now.

Thinking of Melody made those memories of Eve

hazy. Almost thin enough to blow away in a good strong Oklahoma wind.

Melody was something.

When she'd kissed him... She'd obviously been untutored in the art of kissing, but her lips had been a powerful force anyway.

He wanted to do it all over again.

Three days had passed since he'd tucked her into her coupe and bussed her cheek good night. Three nights of waking up from dreams of those kisses. Three mornings watching for her to run past the house. Three mornings of disappointment when she never showed.

He hadn't called. Didn't know if he should. Although some of the younger folks in town accepted him, his reputation could definitely taint her, and he didn't want her store to suffer because of his selfish need to see her again.

But he was about to wave the white flag, because he missed her.

"You should text her."

He jumped at the unexpected voice. He turned his back on the barn out the window he'd been staring out without really seeing to find Chase and Claire behind him. Claire held a pair of bowls and spoons while Chase pulled a tub of ice cream from the freezer.

He started to protest that they couldn't possibly know what he was thinking about, but Claire interrupted. "I think she'd like it if you did. Every time the shop phone rang today, she jumped about a mile. She even fumbled the greeting once."

He scratched the back of his neck, which had suddenly warmed. "You don't think folks would give her a hard time if they saw us together?"

"It's none of their business," Chase growled.

True, but they were quiet in the next moment, and Weston wondered if the girls were thinking the same thing he was, that whether or not it was their business wouldn't stop tongues from wagging.

Something dangerous glinted in Chase's eyes. "If there's not really a curse on our family, you should prove it. Go after her. Make her fall in love with you."

There was just one of the rubs. He didn't know if he could. He hadn't been enough for Eve. Nor for any of his girlfriends since.

Maybe he was cursed.

Except he didn't believe in superstitions. He knew Whose he was. He knew he was loved by the One that really mattered. But that didn't guarantee he'd find someone on earth to love him.

MELODY HAD RESPONDED to Weston's cryptic text with a tentative yes, even though she'd questioned whether his suggestion was wise.

Now, two days later, she wore a long, flowing skirt beneath her coat as she waited for him to pick her up after the store closed.

Tiny snowflakes fell—enough to be beautiful, but not enough to create any road hazards—and his headlights cut through the semi-darkness, making her squint as he pulled the truck into the alley behind the store.

It was a little weird that he'd wanted to pick her up out here.

She started to step off the curb, but he'd already cracked his door and called out, "Wait!"

She froze, one hand against the door.

He rounded the truck and came toward her, his hand closing over hers on the cool metal. "I always open doors."

For women in general, or for his dates?

Before she could speak the question, he was behind her. He pulled the door open, and she backed up to give it room to swing by. But Weston didn't back up, and she was suddenly so close. She didn't move. Standing near him like that, the open door on one side, him on the other, with the light snow falling on their heads...it was a magical moment. An intimate moment.

The shops were deserted this time of night, and the alley was dark and empty, except for the two of them.

She turned toward him and opened her mouth, but before she could speak, he inhaled, nostrils flaring. She watched his eyes sweep down the length of her. His hand slid around her waist, and he pulled her in for a scorching kiss.

When he pulled away—before she was ready, despite the cold wind and snowflakes swirling around them, he tucked her into the cab of the truck with a tiny kiss on the tip of her nose. He was pulling out of the alley and was halfway down Main Street before her wits returned.

"If you meant that you always open the door for your dates, you should know this isn't a date."

He threw a sideways glance at her. "Oh, it's a date. You register for that marathon yet?"

Frustration—and more than a little joy—swirled up through her. "No. And I don't date guys who've seen my scar."

The nearest side of his lips quirked, but he didn't smile. "You mean, like you don't kiss guys who've seen your scar?"

Heat climbed her neck and into her face. "I don't make a habit of kissing anyone at all. Just you."

That glance slid her way again, but this time without any hint of humor. "No kidding?"

WESTON KNEW he was treading on precarious ground as Melody bit her lip, that adorable blush lingering on her cheeks beneath her dark cherry-red locks. He'd been surprised to find her hair color had changed. Not just her bangs this time. The color was cute on her.

He turned toward Weatherford and the surprise he had planned for her.

He'd been her first kiss? She didn't admit it outright, but her silence was confirmation enough.

He'd thought she was out of practice, but would have never guessed that.

"You wanna tell me why?"

She sighed, leaning her cheek on her hand. Her elbow was propped in the window. "Not particularly."

Her opposite hand came up to press against her collarbone.

"Why does the scar bother you so much? It's hardly noticeable."

She frowned, and he fought the urge to take back the words and let her off the hook. Maybe it wasn't typical first-date conversation, but then, she'd already seen some of the darker parts of his family drama.

"It's not like something you'd get from bull riding or sky diving or bike racing," she warned.

Somehow, without really thinking about it, his hand crept across the seat and connected with hers. Their fingers threaded together naturally, and he was gratified when her next words emerged in a less halting manner.

"I had open heart surgery when I was three."

The softly-spoken words hit him square in the gut.

"I had a congenital heart defect, and the surgery repaired it."

He squeezed her hand, but he didn't speak. There was more, he could feel it.

"The doctors told my parents about the risks, of course, but maybe it didn't sink in. I don't know. What-ever the case, there were complications after the surgery. There was a blood clot, and they believe I had a small stroke."

She shook his hand, making him realize he'd been squeezing her too tightly. Imagining the world without Melody in it wasn't something he wanted to do.

"But you're all right now," he said, wanting to believe the words. He needed them to be true.

"I'm fine. I've had more than enough doctor's appointments to confirm it. But because of those weeks spent in the hospital, the scare stuck with my parents. They...basically, they kept me encased in bubble wrap my entire childhood. They schooled me at home. I was never allowed to stay the night with a friend. I wasn't allowed to date."

She hesitated long enough that he glanced at her. Her face was shadowed, but with just the dim lights from the dash for illumination, he saw more that she didn't say. He could only guess what damage her parents' overprotectiveness had caused.

"And then I went to college. I was eighteen, and I'd chosen a state school. I made a stand and told my parents I was going to live in the dorms. My roommate was... she wasn't really wild, but at the time it seemed like she was."

The tension ticked up with every second of her silence. Finally, he said, "And...?"

She glanced at him, and he saw the shadows in her eyes.

"You went with her to the first wild party on campus?" he guessed. "Did some crazy things?"

She drew her hand out of his, and he felt the emptiness of her missing touch as he returned his hand to the steering wheel.

"I locked myself in my dorm for the first week. At first, I couldn't even make myself go to class. I think my roommate wished for a cooler friend. She wasn't trying to be funny when she told me to see a therapist, but her words sparked something in me. I called the campus shrink, and she helped me start working through some issues."

She stared out the passenger window. "I didn't fail that semester after all, even though I had to make up some homework from those first classes I missed."

He could relate to the young woman Melody had been. "College was an adjustment for me, too. Maybe I didn't have it as rough as you did, but being from a small town where everybody knew your business, then transitioning into that big school...it wasn't easy."

He glanced at her again. Was it his imagination, or was she blushing more fiercely now?

"When I got to O State," he said, "I was in the faceless crowd. There was a part of me that liked the anonymity. But another part felt a little lost."

He hadn't meant to share that with her, but there it was.

Thankfully, they arrived at their destination.

She squinted through the windshield, through the snow that had thickened somewhat but was still not enough to cause them trouble on the way home. "Ball-room dancing?"

He popped open his door and ducked into the snow and wind, rounded the truck, and opened her door. She was still peering up at the sign on the building.

He hoped he'd guessed right. "It's gotta be on the list, right?"

CHAPTER 8

*M*elody stepped out of the falling snow and into a warm foyer. Music played. A waltz, maybe.

Glancing around, she took in the colorful paintings hanging on the walls. The foyer was small and opened up into a large, echoing parquet wood floor surrounded by mirrors. The dance floor was well-lit, while the foyer where they stood was lit only by a lamp in the corner.

From across the room, a man stood alone and watched as a couple twirled around the floor, perfectly in sync with each other and the music. Melody recognized some of the movements from her favorite TV show, Dancing with the Stars.

"There's no way I can do that," she muttered.

She hadn't really meant for Weston to hear, but he winked. "How will you know until you try?"

"You haven't seen my klutzy side," she muttered to his back as he moved further into the studio.

The man who'd been watching the dancing couple crossed the room to meet them. "Hello hello."

Before she knew what was happening, the other couple had vacated the floor, and she and Weston were standing under the bright lights with their instructor nearby.

Weston's hands rested loosely at her waist, and both of hers were on his shoulders.

The instructor shook his head. "This is all wrong. You're too tall for her," he told Weston.

Her cheeks burned. Didn't that mean she was too short?

The instructor tapped on Weston's arm. "The hold is all wrong."

"Feels right to me," Weston said, looking down on her with an intensity that only made her blush more.

The instructor huffed. "Maybe for a goodnight kiss, but not for ballroom dancing." He turned to her. "Did you bring any other shoes?"

She shook her head, looking down at her feet. She'd worn ballet flats. She rarely wore even a slight heel.

"That's all right, we've got some extra heels. Size seven?" When she nodded, he disappeared into a room off the corner of the ballroom.

She and Weston traipsed to a small bench along the wall, and she sat down. Their instructor was back before she'd gotten comfortable. He handed her a pair of sparkling sandals with high heels. He then walked off, saying something about restarting the music.

She let the heels dangle from her fingers. She'd never worn heels like that before.

She was aware of Weston's perusal from where he stood several feet away, hands in his pockets as she stared down the shoes.

They were only shoes. But it was more of what they represented.

And then suddenly he was kneeling before her, one warm hand on her ankle as he slipped off her ballet flat. "What are you so nervous about?"

"I might twist my ankle," she replied almost automatically, distracted to the nth degree by his hand on her ankle.

He waited, looking up at her with those bottomless blue eyes. Waiting.

"I might fall," she whispered, and she meant more than fall on her butt in the middle of an empty dance studio.

"I'll catch you," he said.

The moment lengthened between them, almost frozen in time.

Could she trust Weston? Everything inside her screamed yes!

She bent, putting them head to head as she slipped the heels on. She stood, he took her hand, and they joined the instructor on the dance floor. She tried to focus on the instructor as he explained what he wanted them to do, but her glance kept finding Weston's. And then they were moving around the ballroom on the instructor's count.

It wasn't elegant. The simple box step felt awkward at first, more so because she had to move backwards and follow Weston's leading. She had to trust his steps, trust that he wouldn't guide her into a wall or to one of the three support beams throughout the room.

It wasn't in her nature to rely so fully on someone else, not since she'd left home at eighteen.

Was it wrong that she liked it?

She kept her gaze on his face, responded to the small smile that curved his lips.

When their hour was over, she felt exhilarated. She let Weston tuck her into her coat and guide her to the front doors with a hand at her lower back.

"Aren't you glad you tried it?" he asked.

Before she could answer, a gust of wind dragged the door from his hands. Snow blew in over their feet, inciting her to shiver violently.

"Oh no," he muttered.

THIS WAS A DISASTER.

Weston clutched the steering wheel, leaning forward to peer through the snow-clumped windshield until his nose nearly pressed against the glass.

He fought the slick roads, sending up prayer after prayer for their safety, until he had to admit defeat.

After the sixth or seventh time his wheels had slid on black ice buried beneath the snow, he pulled to a stop beneath an overpass.

He beat one palm against the steering wheel and then

looked over to see Melody unclench her white-knuckled grip on the passenger door.

She met his gaze squarely, one eyebrow raised. "I guess we're stuck?"

He pushed a hand through his hair. "I'm really sorry." More than she could know. He bit back an ugly word.

She'd wrapped her coat all the way around her and buttoned up tight when they'd emerged from the dance studio into the falling snow. But she wasn't wearing gloves.

"You warm enough?"

He reached for the heater and turned it up.

"Warm enough. Don't we need to conserve fuel?"

He shook his head. He'd filled up before he'd picked up Melody, and he had an extra five-gallon tank in the back of the pickup that he'd filled up for the tractor. "We've got plenty. Hopefully this will blow on through, and we won't be stuck out here all night."

He'd cut the headlights. He followed her gaze to the circle of light surrounding a streetlamp in the distance, where they could see the snow still falling hard.

"The weatherman only called for a light dusting." He'd checked and double-checked before deciding to make the drive to Weatherford.

"He must've been wrong. It happens."

Yeah, but that didn't stop Weston from kicking himself for the mistake.

He grabbed his phone from the center console. "Do you mind if I call and check on the girls?"

"Of course not." She had her own phone in hand but

she kept looking out the window. He was very aware of their close confines in the cab of the truck. Chase picked up.

"Hey. It snowing there?" he asked.

Her muffled, "It's Weston," must mean she'd told Claire, then her voice rang clear through the connection. "Like a blizzard. Please tell me you stayed in Weatherford."

"That would've been the smart thing to do," he said. "You got the TV on? What does the radar show?"

There was muffled movement through the line, then the sound of the TV in the background.

"Um..."

Okay, that didn't sound promising.

"It's a huge blob. It's going to be snowing for hours."

His chest tightened up.

He glanced over to Melody, who flashed her smartphone at him. The radar showed a huge cloud mass moving slowly over the western part of the state. Where had it come from?

"I want you and Claire to stay inside. I took care of the horses earlier, so there's no reason to go out to the barn. If the electricity goes off, just bundle up, okay? The sleeping bags are in the hall closet."

There was a muffled sound on the phone and then giggles from both of his sisters.

"What?"

"You sound like a worried grandma or something. We'll be fine."

Then the giggling stopped. Chase swallowed audibly

and said, "Thanks," softly. "For taking care of us."

He knew what Mom was like. Knew how, even when she was clean, she sometimes disappeared into herself for days at a time.

He'd been a grown up before he'd hit thirteen. And his sisters, unfortunately, were having the same experience.

"Claire wants to talk to you."

He shifted his phone to his opposite ear. After her greeting, he asked, "You okay?"

"We're fine. We've got While You Were Sleeping on. And the doors are locked."

He smiled into the phone.

"Umm... Mom called."

Something sharp poked the inside of his belly. "Yeah?"

"She said she's coming home in two weeks."

Two weeks. Two weeks left to take care of his sisters. Two weeks with Melody.

It wasn't enough time. Why had he waited so long to make a move? He should've approached her one of the times he'd seen her in town. If they'd been back in the city, he would've.

He cleared his throat, aware of Melody's gaze, aware that Claire was waiting for him to say something. "I'll call her in the morning, make sure her therapist is okay with the release."

Claire didn't respond. What could he say to comfort her? Did she even need comfort? What did he know about teenage girls?

He glanced at Melody. She was looking out the window again, though he didn't know how much she could see with the lights out. In the reflection, he could see she was frowning.

"Everything's going to be okay," he said into the phone. "Tell Chase."

Claire sniffled. "Be careful." She hung up.

He set the phone on the console, gut churning. What had Claire wanted him to say? That he'd stay in town? The girls knew he'd planned to return to the city. It's where his job was. Where his life was.

He'd made a practice of staying gone from Redbud Trails. Told himself the town had nothing for him, even though his sisters were there. But looking over at Melody, he knew that wasn't entirely true. Not anymore.

Weston's lighthearted mood had evaporated when they'd walked out of the studio and into the snowstorm.

She'd suggested they wait out the storm in Weatherford, but he'd summarily dismissed that idea.

And now he seemed even more stressed that they were stuck.

Was he regretting the date? Regretting being with her? He'd softened when he'd talked to his sisters, but then just before he'd hung up, one of the girls had said something that caused a muscle in his jaw to jump.

Now he stared at nothing, his gaze pinpointed on the windshield.

And the woman that had twirled around on the dance floor in Weston's arms had the courage to say, "I'm sorry you're stuck out here with me."

She couldn't help but note the lines around his mouth as he turned and ran his hand through his hair again—a nervous habit? "I'm sorry too."

Okay, she'd been hoping for a denial. For him to say it was no big deal and he was happy for the extra time to spend with her. The charming Weston from earlier would have said something like that.

A shiver wracked her that had nothing to do with cold. Had she been mistaken all this time? Did Weston feel sorry for her, because of her scar and her story? Was that why he'd insisted on the date?

"I'll curl up over here, and you'll never know I'm here," she offered. She'd tried to sound nonchalant, but a little bitterness seeped through.

With her long skirt, she couldn't pull her knees up to her chest like the little girl inside her wanted, but she leaned her elbow against the window and propped her cheek on her fist, closing her eyes.

She felt motion on the seat beside her and then a strong grip around her upper arm.

Her eyes flew open, and she struggled as Weston hauled her into the middle seat.

He still held her arm and from up close, there was nowhere to go, nowhere else to look except at him.

"You think I don't want to be here with you?" he almost-growled.

Her eyes were caught in his intense blues, and she murmured, "You don't seem happy about being stuck," before she'd thought better of it.

"Because I don't want people to connect us."

She saw the words form on his lips, heard them, but didn't understand. "Because...being with me will soil your reputation? Isn't that a little Victorian?"

"Because being with me means people will talk about you. Why do you think I picked you up off the alley?"

"I thought you might want some privacy to kiss me hello," she retorted, her ire rising.

He gave her a look like, yeah, that too.

"I don't care if people know we're on a date." Look at that—she didn't even stumble over the word.

"You might care if some of the women start boycotting your store," he said darkly. Her thigh was pressed against his. He was so near, but as he stared out into the blowing snow, he was distant. "Or if folks suddenly snub you in the supermarket."

She placed her hand on his forearm. He'd shed his coat in the warmth of the cab earlier, and now there was only his cotton shirt between her skin and his. There were such shadows in his eyes.

She laid her hand flat against his jaw, then reached up and kissed him. His lips were warm, and the same spark she felt every time they kissed burned...then flared into a soaring firework that curled throughout her.

He pulled away first, and she laid her head on his shoulder.

"I should be able to stay away from you," he mumbled, but his hand closed over hers and rested on both their thighs.

"I'm glad you haven't."

Then, when he was silent, she said, "You're not eighteen anymore."

She felt the tension spiral through him and rushed on, "You're a successful businessman. You've done well for yourself. Made a new life for yourself."

She felt the rasp of his five o'clock shadow against the fine hairs at her temple as he looked down at her, but she focused her eyes on their linked hands.

"How do you know?"

"The girls respect you. You being here has been good for them. And I might've Googled you."

She felt the muscles of his cheek move against the top of her head. Smiling? But he didn't speak.

She didn't know if she was even making a dent, but something kept her from stopping now. "They can only keep hurting you if you let them."

He exhaled a harsh breath, and his hand tightened around hers.

But he still said nothing.

MELODY NESTLED IN CLOSE, her breaths evening out, though he didn't think she was sleeping.

Holding her close was a comfort, one he probably didn't deserve.

Weston appreciated what Melody was trying to do. For his part, he'd let go of the past as best he could.

He'd loved Eve.

He'd been blindsided when she'd told him she was pregnant—because they'd planned to wait until marriage to sleep together. He'd gone through stages of betrayal and grief. And still planned to marry her. It was the right thing to do.

And because he'd still loved her.

They hadn't told anyone the baby wasn't his. He'd never asked whose it was.

Her family had hated him even as they'd planned a small church wedding for the weekend after graduation. The day of the wedding had come, and Eve had been a no show.

She'd left no note. No phone call. Nothing.

Just left him.

He'd only been in town for two days after that, but the whispers that had followed him around—and that on the heels of what everyone had said about him for weeks —had cut. Every single one.

It was like everyone had forgotten about the first seventeen years of his life. Sure, he'd never been the perfect A student or football hero. He'd made his share of trouble, but he hadn't been the pariah that people had come to believe he was those final weeks of his senior year.

He couldn't get away from town fast enough.

And now his mom was getting out of rehab. He should be racing away from here, away from folks like Ezra, who still had it out for him.

But instead, he looked at Melody's head where she pillowed her cheek against his shoulder, and wished.

CHAPTER 9

"*I*t's still not right!"

Claire's wailed words—on top of all the drama of the past two days—caused a throbbing pain behind Weston's right eye.

He needed an ibuprofen. Or to escape this madhouse.

With two weeks until Valentine's Day, why had he let the three women talk him into this?

Melody touched his calf—about the only part she could reach from where he stood on a six-foot ladder—and the pain almost went away. Almost

"A little to the left, and we'll call it good, right girls? You still have to get dressed, too."

Arms aching, he tied off the heart-shaped paper lantern and got the heck off the ladder before Claire changed her mind again.

Claire and Chase rushed out of the barn, their low tones muttering something about makeup, leaving him to put away the ladder.

When he emerged from the storage room at the back of the barn, he stood for a moment and watched Melody —whose hair color was now auburn—plug in the white twinkle lights they'd strung in a criss-crossed pattern beneath the high barn ceiling. They all lit up, thank God, and didn't blow the fuse.

That might change when Chase plugged in the stereo for whatever dance music—or what passed for it—they'd start in about an hour when the guests arrived.

He'd been skeptical when Melody suggested they host a party for the freshman class a week before the official school Valentine's Day. A dozen fourteen- and fifteen-year-old teens on his property?

But Melody had insisted the two of them could chaperone, and Claire and Chase would still get to have the dance they'd been denied, thanks to Ezra Warren.

He was in love with this creative, beautiful woman.

And he was still leaving.

He rested his hand on the empty stall where one of Ben's two rescued mares had stayed until the day before, when Ben had come out to relocate them. They'd been a lot of work, but Weston had seen improvement in their temperaments and their trust in humans in the short weeks he'd cared for them. The girls had been smitten with them.

He kinda missed how they snuffled his jacket for treats.

He was going to miss a lot of things from Redbud Trails. Melody. The girls.

His mom's therapist seemed to think she was in a

good place for her release. She was expected sometime next week.

And then he'd have no reason not to get back to his life, back to his job in Oklahoma City.

He and Melody had tiptoed around the issue of his leaving since they'd made it back from Weatherford. The storm had cleared out after several hours. Melody had fallen asleep on his chest, and he'd been loathe to wake her up, but he also didn't want her neighbors worrying—and gossiping—if she were out all night.

He'd driven about ten miles an hour, and the trip back to Redbud Trails had taken five times what it normally would have, but he'd delivered Melody home before daybreak.

He hadn't been able to stay away from her in the two weeks since.

She'd surprised him with an indoor picnic supper one night—which the girls had crashed, but that was okay.

He'd gone to her house after the store closed a couple of nights to watch movies and eat a late supper.

He hadn't been hiding the fact that they were sort of dating—mostly due to Melody's insistence—but he also hadn't been broadcasting it around town.

He didn't want anyone making trouble for Melody, especially since he was leaving.

"You're looking awfully serious, cowboy." Melody strode close, looking adorable as usual in her denim skirt and a tall pair of pink cowgirl boots.

He didn't want to talk about leaving, not when this might be one of the last times he had her alone.

"You said you never went to a school dance?" he asked instead, reaching for her and letting his hands settle at her waist.

"Nope." She followed his lead as he mostly swayed in the silence.

"This is a little different from the box step we learned," she said.

His chin brushed her temple; he could hear the smile in her voice.

"This was my repertoire in high school." He nuzzled his nose into her hair. "In fact, don't be surprised if we turn on the music and the boys huddle on one side of the barn and the girls stick to the opposite. I don't think I asked a girl to dance until..."

He shook his head. What was he thinking, bringing up Eve?

The shock of pain that normally accompanied thoughts of his high school girlfriend was noticeably absent. He could thank Melody for that.

She'd been a huge help as he'd dealt with the girls. And he knew she'd stay in their lives after he left, now that they both worked part-time in her shop.

The sound of a horn honking had him releasing Melody and moving out of the barn's double doors so he could see the drive.

"Don't tell me someone's an hour early," Melody was saying from behind him, but his hearing had gone to a high-pitched hum.

"It's my mom."

Melody accompanied Weston into the house—he'd clutched her hand and hadn't let go, so she'd really had no choice but to follow him in. Not that she would have been anywhere else.

They made it to the kitchen just as the front door opened and a woman with gray hair and features that identified her as Weston and the girls' mother pushed through the front door. She carried a large duffel that she set just inside the door.

"Weston."

"Mom."

The older woman's eyes tracked along Weston's arm to where their hands were clasped. Melody stepped forward. "Hello. I'm Melody."

"I recognize you."

Weston squeezed her hand gently. "This is my mother. Karly Moore."

"Melody, is that you? We need advice on our eye shadow..." Claire's exuberant voice faded as she walked from the hall and right into the middle of the tension-filled family living area.

"What—?" Chase bumped into Claire's back, then went silent too.

"What are you wearing?" Karly asked. No hello to the girls.

Claire had the audacity to prop a hand on her hip, showing off the designer dress she'd earned through working at the store. Beside her, Chase moved slightly into the living room so that her skinny jeans and a rainbow-hued long sleeved T-shirt were visible, along with the trendy short boots Melody had let her borrow from her own closet.

"We're having an early Valentine's Day party," Claire said, her chin raised in what was almost a dare.

Karly slid a glance to Weston. "I guess your brother's paying for your new clothes and a party? Don't get used to it."

"Mom," Weston started.

"Actually, we bought the clothes," Chase piped in. "We both got jobs."

Karly's eyes narrowed, and she threw an accusing glance at Weston. "Your brother let you get jobs?"

"Maybe we can talk about it after you get settled in," Weston suggested.

Claire threw a pleading glance at Melody.

"Eye shadow. Right." Melody let go of Weston's hand, instantly missing the contact, and started to follow the girls to their room.

"Let me get that for you, Mom," Weston said.

She glanced over her shoulder to see Weston grabbing his mom's duffel bag. "My stuff's in your room, but it won't take me long to pack up."

Melody's stomach dipped to her toes, her heart catching up with her head on what exactly it meant that Karly had returned.

Weston would be leaving. Soon.

"She wasn't supposed to be home until Tuesday," Chase murmured when Melody followed the girls into their room.

They both sat on their beds, and the emotional look

they shared said everything. They weren't thrilled to have their mom home. Weston and the girls had settled into a comfortable rhythm, and now, everything would change.

It made Melody a little sick to her stomach, knowing the girls must be wondering when or if Karly would go off the deep end again.

"Things are different now," Melody said. The space between the twin beds was close enough that she could reach out and touch both twins' shoulders. "You'll still see me three afternoons a week and more during the summer." And she made a silent vow that if she saw any signs that Karly was self-medicating, she'd contact Weston.

"Maybe," Chase said darkly. Melody could only hope that Karly would let the girls keep their jobs. It might ease some of the money troubles and allow them to gain some independence. And they thrived in the work.

"And Weston is only a phone call away," Melody added.

"Yeah." Claire's agreement was half-hearted, and she stared down at her fingers, which were twisting a loose thread on her bedspread.

Melody squeezed their shoulders lightly. "It'll be okay."

Claire slid a sideways look at Melody. "We thought Weston might want to stay. In Redbud Trails."

"He likes you," Chase added. "A lot."

She liked him a lot too. Thinking about him leaving opened a gaping hole inside her.

"Would you...ask him to stay?"

She bit her lip and shook her head slightly. She'd stayed up nights thinking about what things could be like if Weston chose to stay in town. But she also knew how hard it was for him to be here.

She could never ask him to stay, knowing that his past caused him pain, and that some folks wouldn't let him forget it.

Even if her heart was breaking.

"Let's get your eye shadow right," she said, injecting a positive tone into her voice. "Your friends will be here before you know it."

The girls looked at each other, pink showing in their cheeks before their eyes started dancing once again.

Crisis averted, at least until after the party.

WESTON STOOD with his arms crossed in the shadows at the back of the barn. Brooding maybe, but he couldn't help it.

His mom was home early. And her return had already caused tension with the twins.

What would happen when he was gone? He wouldn't be nearby to watch over them. What if his mom got depressed again? Started using again? Who would be there for the twins?

Melody would.

He knew she'd call him in the city if he needed to come home.

But he ached, thinking about being two and a half hours from her instead of only a few minutes away.

"You're scaring the guests." Melody joined him. She'd been in her element for the last hour, greeting the guests with Claire and Chase.

His sisters cleaned up nice. They were beaming, wafting from group to group like grown up butterflies or something.

That was Melody's doing, not his.

"About half of them need to be scared." He nodded toward a crowd of boys. "Scared is good."

A commotion near the wide open barn doors had several of the teens' heads turning in that direction. Chase, who was standing a couple of yards away with three other girls, gasped audibly.

Three boys stood in the open doorway, looking uncomfortable and out of place.

Whispers traveled through the groups of kids. No one made a move to greet them, as if everyone was frozen, watching.

Melody whispered something to herself.

"What?" he asked.

"It's him. Jeremy."

He shrugged, palms raised.

"Jeremy." She huffed a sigh at him. "The guy Chase has been crushing on."

Suddenly, it registered. Jeremy Warren. Ezra's son.

"He's not a freshman," Weston muttered.

"No. He isn't."

The sophomore was in the middle of two other young

men friends who must've been there for support. As Weston watched, he straightened his shoulders and strode into the barn.

Right through the clusters of freshmen and straight up to Weston.

"Jeremy Warren."

Weston shook the kid's hand. He had to give him props. The kid met his eyes, unflinching, and had a firm handshake.

"I hope it's okay that I crashed the party." Now there was red creeping up his neck from the collar of his plaid button-up. "I really wanted to invite Chase to the Valentine's dance, but my dad..." He glanced to the side, where Chase had moved two steps away from her friends, obviously listening in, even over the loud music blaring.

"My buddies and I are boycotting the school dance," Jeremy said, loud enough that Chase could hear too.

"Does your dad know you're here?" Weston asked.

Jeremy nodded, unsmiling. "He wasn't too happy about it, but I had to make a stand." Another covert—or not so much—glance at Chase.

What could Weston say, if the kid was brave enough to stand up to his own dad to come and hang out with Chase?

"And just for the record, I don't agree with the way my dad's been treating you, either."

It was all Weston could do to nod. His throat had gone suspiciously tight.

Melody squeezed Weston's arm. "Have fun at the party, Jeremy."

Weston nodded to the kid. Before he'd even turned away, Chase was there, asking shyly, "Do you want to dance?"

They joined the four or five kids who were—awkwardly—dancing in the middle of the floor. Jeremy's buddies mingled.

Weston saw Chase shoot a wide-eyed glance at Claire, who returned a double thumbs up when Jeremy wasn't looking.

Chase had gotten her happy ending.

And he had to appreciate the kid's guts in coming tonight, standing up to his father.

Had Weston been wrong all this time? Could people really forget and move on?

Was he reading too much into Ezra's actions?

He didn't know.

What he did know was that now that Karly was home, he didn't have a place to sleep. It would be a late drive home to his empty apartment in Oklahoma City.

Melody settled one arm around his waist and he slid his arm around her shoulder. Holding her for maybe the last time.

He didn't want to say goodbye.

But he didn't have a choice.

CHAPTER 10

A week later, Melody unlocked the front door of the store for Anna and Lila. An unusual early-morning fog hid most of Main Street from view.

"Your hair," Anna gasped.

Melody tucked a strand of straight, brown hair behind her ear self-consciously as her friends trooped inside the store. This was all her. Her normal color and the boring straight locks she'd been born with.

Lila was behind Anna on the stoop of Melody's store, but she was the one to push inside. "What did you do to yourself? Is this some sign of depression?"

After Anna joined them, Melody locked the door and took the cup of coffee from Anna's fingers.

"Remember when you started wearing your hair down?" Melody asked Lila.

The other woman's eyes widened. She'd stopped wearing her hair in tight French braids and buns when she'd fallen for Ben and admitted that she didn't have to try so hard to control everything in her life.

"You fell for Weston," Anna said.

Melody couldn't say it aloud. It hurt too much, now that he was gone.

"Come on back," she said instead. "The last alterations to your dress are finished, and you'll want to see it on."

She set her coffee on the front counter, safely away from the dressing rooms, and began unzipping the large white garment bag she'd hung on the tall rack late last night.

"One week to go," Lila said. "Any thoughts of backing out?"

"None," said Anna as she fingered one lacy fold of the dress. "I'm happier than I have been in a long time."

Melody was glad for her friend. Anna had grieved her first husband and had worked hard to provide for her children. She deserved someone like Kelly to pamper her and love her back.

But it was very hard not to be jealous.

Instead, she shored up her courage and said, "I wanted to tell you...if you want to change back to the peach dress—the one with the sweetheart neckline—I'm okay with that."

Both Lila and Anna turned, almost in sync, and stared at her. She couldn't blame them and suppressed the blush that wanted to rise.

This morning, she'd faced her mirrored reflection as she'd been dressing and stared down the scar. She couldn't help remembering Weston's words, that her scar was a badge of courage. She missed him so much.

Was she the woman who'd braved heels to take dancing lessons? The woman who would run a marathon later in the spring?

Or was she a coward, hiding behind fear and crew necks?

She'd donned a sweater with a square-cut neckline that she'd never dared wear before. And she hadn't tried to disguise it with jewelry or a scarf.

"Mel," Anna breathed. She dropped the fabric of the gown and threw her arms around Melody. Lila joined in the embrace, putting her arms around both of them.

Melody couldn't stop her eyes from filling with tears. She sniffed, valiantly attempting to stem the flow, but it was no use.

"Oh, honey," Lila comforted her, patting her back.

Anna let go of Melody, fished through her purse, and retrieved some tissues. She pressed them into Melody's hand. "Have you heard from him?"

Melody shook her head. "I told him..." Her voice wavered, and she had to take a breath before she could finish. "I told him a clean break was better. I thought it would be easier not to try and keep things going long distance."

"Well, that was dumb." But Lila patted her shoulder.

Melody wiped at her tears with the tissues. "I know. I should've told him I would take anything—long distance, sell the store and move to OKC..."

Anna snorted. "You can't sell your shop. You love it too much."

She did. But she also loved Weston.

"Why don't you just call him?" Anna asked gently. Anna had come around after Melody revealed what she could about Weston's past without invading his privacy.

She'd thought about calling him. But even though she was learning to be brave, it was still scary. She dabbed at the tears that were finally drying up. "Maybe I will."

She tossed the used tissues. "Today isn't about me. We've got to get you in that dress and make sure it fits."

She accepted one more hug from each of her friends. She couldn't let Weston's absence ruin Anna's day. The wedding would be here in a week, and then she could decide what to do.

"THIS SEAT TAKEN?"

Melody startled at the familiar, warm voice behind her.

She twisted in her seat at the head table to find Weston standing there.

"Hey." He cracked his trademark half smile, and she pushed back the chair, stood, and threw herself into his arms.

He caught her and buried his nose in the crown of her updo.

"What are you doing here?" Her words were muffled in his chest, the soft linen of his shirt and tie. His jacket enveloped her bare arms as she hugged him around the waist.

She took back the question. It didn't matter what he was doing there, just that he was.

"Can I steal you away for a minute?"

She glanced around the half-empty multi-purpose room of the church. The bride and groom hadn't finished their pictures, and wedding guests were still meandering in.

Lila looked from where she and Ben were embracing, half-hidden by a potted plant caddy-corner from the door. She made a shooing motion with one hand, urging Melody to disappear with Weston.

Melody didn't need to be told twice.

He took her hand and led her out of the large room, down the hall, and into an empty adult classroom.

He pulled her into his arms before the door had even clicked closed and greeted her with a searing kiss. His hands were in her hair—thank goodness they'd taken all the bridesmaid pictures earlier—and the mass tumbled out of its pins and down around her shoulders.

"I missed you," he said when he finally broke the kiss.

"I can tell." She couldn't stop smiling.

"What's this?" he asked, running one hand through her straight brown hair. "No color?"

She bit her lip and shook her head slightly. "This is...the real me."

His finger traced her collarbone, where the sweetheart neckline of the bridesmaid dress did nothing to hide her scar. "And this?"

"Still the real me." She ran her hands across his shoulders, reassuring herself that he was really here. "And I registered for the Memorial marathon." The annual Oklahoma City event was always in late April and that gave her about six weeks to finish her training.

"I'll drive down and cheer you across the finish line," he said, brushing a kiss across her cheek.

He believed she could do it. The knowledge warmed her from the inside.

And then his words registered.

"Drive down?" Suddenly, her heart was beating in her throat.

"Yeah. It'll mean getting up early, but I can deal."

"Drive down from where?" She leaned away when he tried to distract her with another kiss.

"I sold my condo," he said. "I'm relocating."

She waited, holding her breath.

"Here." He seemed to wait, a small note of uncertainty in the depths of his eyes.

"Thank goodness." She closed her eyes against the relieved tears that threatened to overwhelm her. One slipped out, and he brushed it away with his thumb.

"So that's a happy tear?" he whispered.

She nodded, eyes still closed. "Now I don't have to sell my shop."

He laughed.

He replaced his thumb with his lips and then slowly moved the kiss from her cheek down to her lips.

She gave him a proper welcome home until they were both breathless.

He pressed her close to his chest. She clung to his waist, holding him tightly.

"Have you told the twins?"

"I called them on my way up here, but I had to see you first."

"I bet they're excited."

He chuckled. "Seemed like it. They probably just want me to chaperone some more parties for them."

"Oh, it's only starting with them," she teased. "Soon, they'll be dating."

He groaned. "I don't want to think about that right now."

He rested his forehead against hers. "I only want to think about us."

She liked the sound of that.

"I was wondering if there was something else we could mark off your list. Something big."

Her heart thudded against her ribs. She licked her lips. "Like what?"

One of his hands let go of her waist, and he reached into his pocket. He raised a small black velvet-covered box into her line of sight, and suddenly she couldn't breathe.

"Something big," he repeated. "Melody, I want our life to be an adventure together. Will you marry me?"

"Yes. Yes, yes!"

His eyes sparkled with unshed tears, and she was gratified that she wasn't the only one overflowing with emotion.

"You haven't even seen the ring yet," he said with a chuckle.

"It doesn't matter what it looks like. It's the man attached to the ring I'm interested in."

But that didn't stop her from gasping over the huge emerald-cut diamond that sparkled under the overhead lights.

Noise from the door interrupted their interlude, and suddenly Chase and Claire were barging in. "Lila told us you snuck off somewhere."

"We found you!"

The girls oohed and aahed over the ring and embraced the both of them, and then Lila and Ben were crowding inside, and Kelly and Anna in her glamorous wedding dress.

And Melody beamed up at Weston all the while.

Her prince charming had come back for her.

And their happy ending was just right.

<<<<>>>>

ALSO BY LACY WILLIAMS

WILD WYOMING HEART SERIES (HISTORICAL ROMANCE)

Marrying Miss Marshal

Counterfeit Cowboy

Cowboy's Pride

Courted by the Cowboy

TRIPLE H BRIDES SERIES (CONTEMPORARY ROMANCE)

Kissing Kelsey

Courting Carrie

Stealing Sarah

Keeping Kayla

COWBOY FAIRYTALES SERIES (CONTEMPORARY ROMANCE)

Once Upon a Cowboy

Cowboy Charming

The Toad Prince

The Beastly Princess

The Lost Princess

NOT IN A SERIES

Love's Glimmer

How to Lose a Guy in 10 Dates

Santa Next Door

The Butterfly Bride

Secondhand Cowboy

Wagon Train Sweetheart (historical romance)

Made in the USA
Coppell, TX
22 October 2021